THOUSAND OAKS LIBRARY

2053 01239 9252

AUG 2017

DISCARD

P9-DMO-464

PROPERTY OF
THOUSAND OAKS LIBRARY
1401 E. Janss Road
Thousand Oaks, California

For my parents

A FEIWEL AND FRIENDS BOOK
An imprint of Macmillan Publishing Group, LLC

DON'T BLINK! Copyright © 2017 by Tom Booth. All rights reserved.
Printed in China by RR Donnelley Asia Printing Solutions Ltd., Dongguan City, Guangdong Province.
For information, address Feiwel and Friends, 175 Fifth Avenue, New York, N.Y. 10010.

Our books may be purchased in bulk for promotional, educational, or business use. Please contact your local
bookseller or the Macmillan Corporate and Premium Sales Department at (800) 221-7945 ext. 5442 or by e-mail at
MacmillanSpecialMarkets@macmillan.com.

Library of Congress Cataloging-in-Publication Data is available.

ISBN 978-1-250-11736-6

Book design by Tom Booth, Rich Deas, and Eileen Savage

Feiwel and Friends logo designed by Filomena Tuosto

First Edition—2017

The artwork was created using a combination of traditional and digital techniques. Tom begins by illustrating
characters and environments in ink, graphite, charcoal, or gouache. He then scans those early sketches so he can
redraw and refine his illustrations in the computer, using digital brushes and other tools in Photoshop.

1 3 5 7 9 10 8 6 4 2   jj Fiction

mackids.com

DON'T BLINK!

TOM BOOTH

Feiwel and Friends
New York

Are you ready?

On your mark . . .

Get set . . .

Go!

Excuse me, what are you doing?

I'm having a staring contest.

Hello there.

Stay strong, everyone.
Keep those eyes open.

DON'T BLINK, DON'T BLINK,
DON'T BLINK, DON'T BLINK!

I think YOU won!

I'm going to start a staring
contest of my own!